Squiggly's Race to the Ark

Written by Tim Davis
Art by Kenny DeWitt

Would you like to know how your child is gifted?
Get Your FREE Copy of Squiggly's Gift Assessment
on our website
www.SquigglyAndFriends.com

This is the story of Squiggly the Snail. Squiggly dreamed of doing something great with his life. His parents told him that he had special gifts and that God had great plans for him!

But no matter how much his parents encouraged him, the other animals made fun of him, and their words made him sad.

Some said, "Squiggly, you're too slow!"

Others told him, "Squiggly, you leave a slimy trail everywhere you go."

But there were three animals who became friends to Squiggly. They were Samantha, who was another snail, and Galen and Grace, who were grasshoppers.

One day, Galen came hopping and shouting, "Hurry, Squiggly, we have to go! God is sending a great flood, and Noah built an Ark for the animals. We have to go in pairs, two by two."

"Why would God want me?" Squiggly wondered aloud. "I'm slow, and I leave a slimy trail everywhere I go."

"God called you, Squiggly. You have to go!" said Galen. "Go get Samantha. Grace and I will go ahead and meet you on the Ark."

"Is this really true, Galen?" asked Squiggly.

"It's true. Dael, the wise old owl, told me. Now, hurry up! It's a long journey to the Ark," replied Galen.

Then Squiggly believed, because he knew that Dael was very wise. In fact, the name Dael means "the knowledge of God."

Squiggly had to make a decision. Should he stay or go to the Ark?

He worried that he was too slow and that the other animals would make fun of his slimy trail. What was he going to do?

Squiggly found Samantha and told her all that Galen had said about the Ark. He also shared his fears about making the journey.

"Squiggly!" Samantha exclaimed. "God has created us for a purpose. If He has called us to the Ark, then we must go. God will help us along the way. Our job is simply to start the journey!"

So, Samantha and Squiggly started their journey to the Ark.

Although they had to travel a long way, each day Squiggly and Samantha encouraged each other that they could make it to the Ark before the flood.

Then one day, they ran into trouble. Slither the Snake came out from behind a rock to scare them. "Where are you going?" Slither asked.

"God is sending a great flood and has called us to go to the Ark that Noah built before the flood comes," Squiggly said nervously.

"Hogwash!" hissed Slither.
"You don't really believe that lie, do you? And besides, you are way too slow to make it before the flood anyway!"

"Maybe Slither is right,"
Squiggly thought sadly to himself.

Suddenly, Dusty, the bald eagle, swooped down! He looked directly at Slither and asked, "What is going on here?"

Very scared by Dusty, Slither stuttered, "Oh nothing, nothing at all. I am just talking with my friends, Samantha and Squiggly."

"Is this true?" Dusty asked Squiggly.

"We were headed to the Ark, but Slither said it was a lie and God isn't sending a flood," answered Squiggly.

"How dare you lie to Samantha and Squiggly!" yelled Dusty as he raised his feathers. Turning and pointing at Slither, he shouted, "Get out of here and leave them alone!"

Samantha and Squiggly were so scared they went into their shells.

Dusty turned, tapped on Squiggly's shell, and said, "You can come out now. There is nothing to be afraid of. God has called you and will continue to help you and Samantha on your journey to the Ark."

Squiggly and Samantha thanked Dusty for his help and continued on their way.

The days in the desert were very hot, and the journey seemed so very long. But, day by day, Squiggly and Samantha continued on. At night, they rested and talked with each other about their journey.

Finally, as they came near the top of a large hill, they sensed something different. As they reached the top, Squiggly peeked over and saw Noah's Ark in the valley. He and Samantha were filled with excitement as they realized they were almost there.

Samantha looked
at Squiggly and said,
"All we need to do is
slide down this hill, and
we'll be at the Ark!"

They slid down the hill, laughing
with joy as they thought about
seeing Noah and all of the animals
safely on the Ark.

However, after they boarded the Ark, Squiggly was shocked that many of the animals had not yet arrived. He asked Noah, "How did we make it to the Ark before everyone else?"

Noah replied, "I don't know, Squiggly. But don't worry. God will make a way for them, just as He made one for you."

Although Noah said not to, Squiggly couldn't help but worry about the animals who had not made it to the Ark, even the ones who had been mean to him.

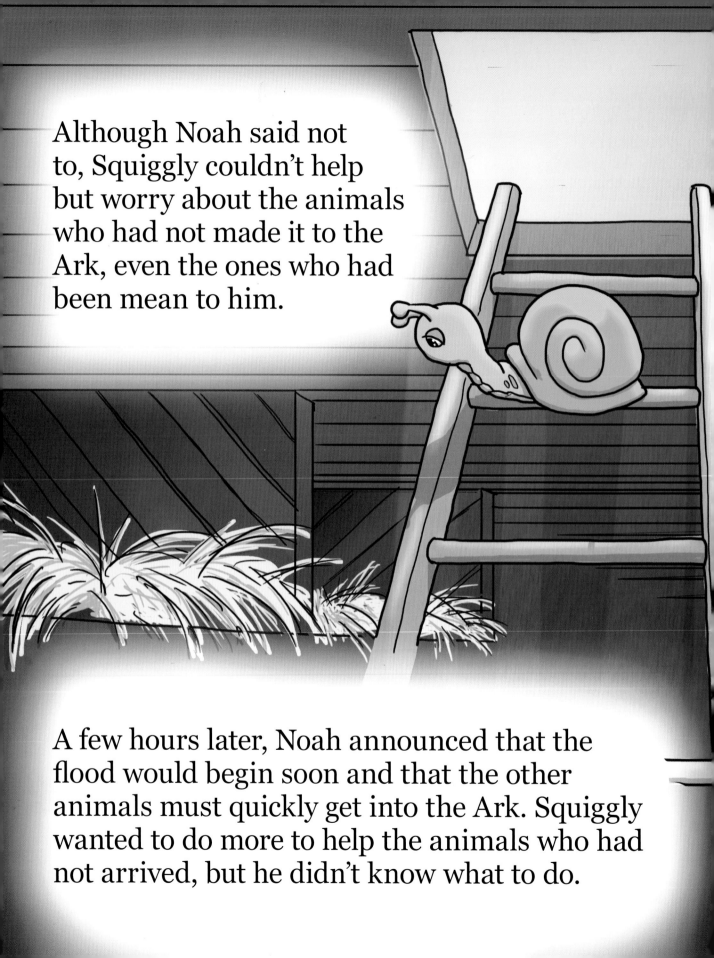

A few hours later, Noah announced that the flood would begin soon and that the other animals must quickly get into the Ark. Squiggly wanted to do more to help the animals who had not arrived, but he didn't know what to do.

Suddenly, there was a loud noise outside the Ark. "Squiggly! Samantha!" shouted Noah. "Come look outside!"

As Squiggly and Samantha looked outside, they saw Galen, Grace, and all of the other animals rushing to the Ark. They watched with excitement as the animals boarded the Ark, two by two.

Just as everyone was finally on board, the flood came and the Ark began to float.

Noah was so happy. He looked at Dael, the wise old owl, and said, "All of the animals made it just in time. What caused them to be so late?"

Dael explained, "Many of them got lost on their journey. Then one day, the sun was very bright and began shining off Squiggly's slimy trail. The animals saw the reflection and began to follow the trail."

Noah looked at Squiggly and said,
"It was your trail that helped those
who were lost find their way!"

Everyone was so excited
that God had used
Squiggly in such
a great way!

Squiggly finally realized that God had given him everything he needed to be the best snail he could be. And the slimy trail that Squiggly didn't like—because it made him different—was actually a gift that made him special and helped others find their way.

And the cool thing is . . . God has a special purpose for you and has given you special gifts to help others, too!

A Word To Parents

"What do you want to be when you grow up?"

How many of us were asked this question when we were children? In fact, how many people do you know right now in their 30's, 40's, or even older who still ponder this question?

The truth is, if someone doesn't help us identify our gifts when we are children, it becomes harder and harder for us to identify them the older we get.

My story: I grew up in the projects and, while I knew my mother loved me and raised me in the best way she knew, she didn't really know how to recognize my gifts at an early age. I ended up on a long, sometimes-fun-and-sometimes-lonely journey, as I struggled to find my gifts and my life's purpose on my own. And, I'm afraid my story happens all too often, each and every day.

That is why you can get Squiggly's God-Given Gift Assessment absolutely FREE! Go to www.SquigglyandFriends.com and click the Gift Assessment link. This resource will help you identify, encourage, and nurture your children to grow in their gifts and talents.

I think it is every parent's responsibility to help his children recognize their gifts and provide them guidance and opportunities to grow in those gifts. That is why I wrote this book. Simply put, God wants our best and has equipped us for special works!

I hope this book has been a blessing and encouragement to you. I pray that God will reveal to you, your family, and your children how fearfully and wonderfully you are made! I also believe the gifts God has given you will be used in a mighty way . . . just like Squiggly's.

Train up a child in the way he should go: and when he is old, he will not depart from it.

~ Proverbs 22:6